GA

SUPER
SIDE
KICKS

Ocean's
Revenge

PUFFIN

PUFFIN BOOKS

UK | USA | Canada | Ireland | Australia
India | New Zealand | South Africa

Puffin Books is part of the Penguin Random House group of companies
whose addresses can be found at global.penguinrandomhouse.com.

www.penguin.co.uk
www.puffin.co.uk
www.ladybird.co.uk

First published in Australia by Penguin Random House Australia Pty Ltd 2019
Published in Great Britain by Puffin Books 2021

001

Copyright © Gavin Aung Than, 2019

The moral right of the author has been asserted

Cover and internal design by Gavin Aung Than and Benjamin Fairclough
© Penguin Random House Australia Pty Ltd

Printed and bound in Great Britain by Clays Ltd, Elcograf S.p.A

The authorized representative in the EEA is Penguin Random House Ireland,
Morrison Chambers, 32 Nassau Street, Dublin D02 YH68

A CIP catalogue record for this book is available from the British Library

ISBN: 978–0–241–43489–5

All correspondence to:
Puffin Books
Penguin Random House Children's
One Embassy Gardens,
8 Viaduct Gardens
London SW11 7BW

Penguin Random House is committed to a
sustainable future for our business, our readers
and our planet. This book is made from Forest
Stewardship Council® certified paper.

PREVIOUSLY . . .

Four superhero sidekicks were sick of being bullied by their selfish grown-up partners, so they decided to form their own team. They are the

SUPER SIDEKICKS!

JUNIOR JUSTICE (JJ to his friends)

Born leader. Expert martial artist. Brilliant detective. Assisted by Ada, the world's most advanced belt buckle.

FLYGIRL

Acrobatic flyer. Bug whisperer. Cricket lover (the sport and the insect). Uses dangerous bug balls to subdue enemies.

DINOMITE

Dinosaur shapeshifter. Physics professor. Poetry connoisseur. Would rather be reading a book.

GOO

Limitless stretch factor. Untapped power potential. Still has nightmares about his past as a bad guy.

THE GROWN-UPS

Captain Perfect, the world's most beloved (and obnoxious) superhero; **Rampagin' Rita**, simple yet scary strong; and **Blast Radius**, who hasn't met a problem he couldn't solve by blowing it up.

Chapter

They are, in fact, **littered** with trash – **OUR** trash.

Millions of tonnes of the world's junk end up here . . .

. . . **The Great Pacific Rubbish Patch.**

A giant whirlpool of rubbish soup the size of a small country.

And what makes up most of it?

Plastic, plastic and **more plastic!**

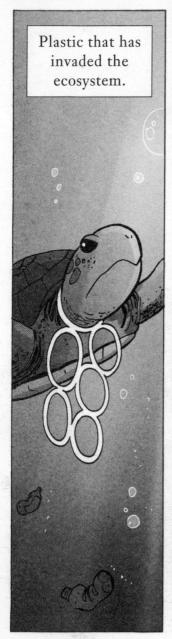

Plastic that has invaded the ecosystem.

Plastic that wreaks havoc on marine wildlife.

Plastic that will never, **ever** go away.

6

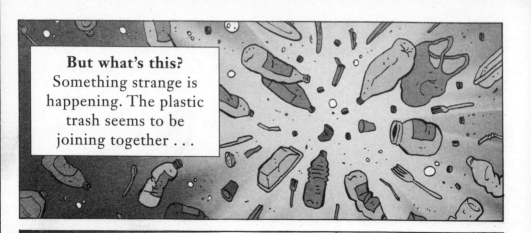

But what's this? Something strange is happening. The plastic trash seems to be joining together . . .

It's miraculously combining to form **bigger and bigger** pieces.

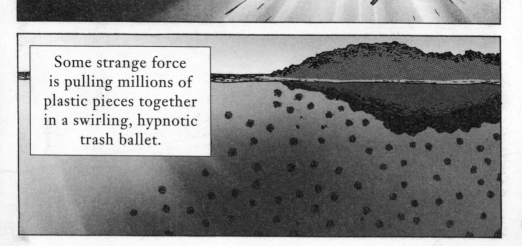

Some strange force is pulling millions of plastic pieces together in a swirling, hypnotic trash ballet.

At last, all of the trash from the Great Pacific Rubbish Patch has been concentrated into one giant **plastic super-cluster.**

The island crackles and pops with a violent energy.

Wait. It can't be.

It's not possible! The plastic island . . . it . . .

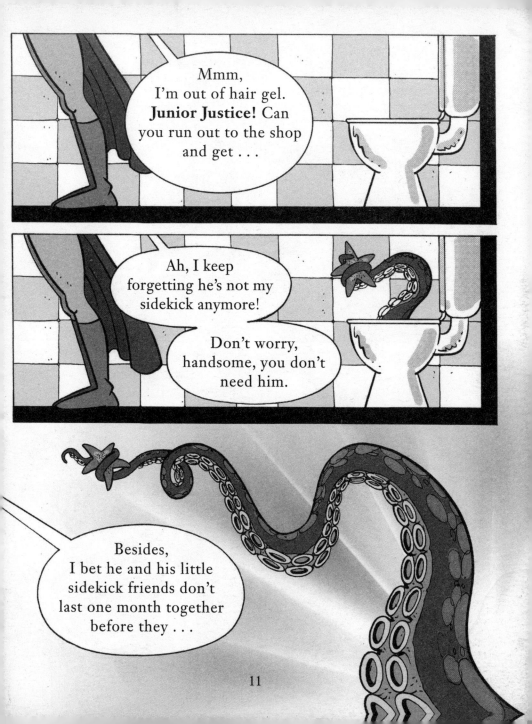

11

– away
with this.

14

All over the world, earth's superheroes are being taken out.

Star Knight is the next to go.

Mother Bear gets surprised while on holiday in Siberia.

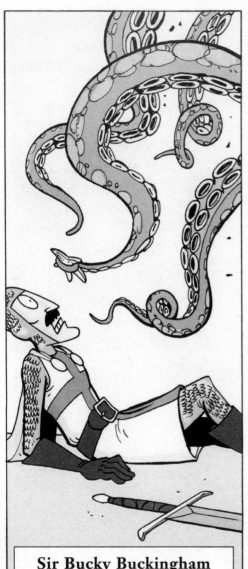

Sir Bucky Buckingham
doesn't stand a chance
against this mysterious foe.

Heroine **Bellatrix**
gets taken while fying
over the Amazon River.

Old Man Dragon falls prey to the tentacle attack.

And finally, **Lucie Liberté** gets dragged into the sewer system!

And just like that, the planet's first line of defence is gone . . .

MISSING
Earth's Greatest Superheroes

CAPTAIN PERFECT

RAMPAGIN' RITA

BLAST RADIUS

STAR KNIGHT

MOTHER BEAR

SIR BUCKY BUCKINGHAM

BELLATRIX

OLD MAN DRAGON

LUCIE LIBERTÉ

Who will protect us now?

Chapter

May I ask what your fascination is with them?

Just between you and me, Ada, **clowns give me the creeps.**

Sifu* taught me one should **always face their fear head-on.** The more I train against them, the less scared I get.

* A Cantonese word meaning 'martial arts teacher'.

Is it working?

Yeah, I think I'm making some real . . .

AHHH!

I'll reset the same opponents for tomorrow, shall I?

Very funny.

30

Well, 'beautiful' is when something is nice-looking. A person can be beautiful on the **inside** too.

Or when something is just soooooo pretty it makes you feel all **warm** and **fuzzy** inside. Mmm, like a **Goliath Bird-Eating Spider.**

Like Flygirl. Flygirl beautiful!

Aw, thanks, you **beautiful** pink blob!

Why Flygirl teach Goo reading?

Cos you need to be a good reader to learn about, well . . . **everything!**

Books are filled with all the knowledge in the world. You need some of that since you're not a prisoner in Dr Enok's lab any more.*

* Goo was created by the evil Dr Enok, as seen in SUPER SIDEKICKS book 1!

Yay! **Knowww-led-ge.**

And books can be full of **amazing** stories that transport you to **fantastical** places where you get to meet **incredible** characters!

Woooaaaah.

Thank you for helping Goo. Goo happy here. Goo happy to be **Super Sidekick.**

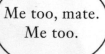

Me too, mate. Me too.

33

GULP

I've been looking for him **everywhere!**

Lucky you didn't chew on him, JJ. Giant Centipedes are pretty feisty. My mate Sebastian here would have given your tongue a nasty bite.

How many times do I have to tell you, Flygirl? Please, *PLEEEASE* keep your door closed.

SLURP!

None of us want to accidentally eat one of your **gross bugs!**

MUNCH MUNCH

Isn't that right, Goo?

Mmm—hmm.

IT'S READY!

The **SSSDSC** scans the world for all possible threats and alerts us to what needs our immediate attention. It's a triumph of **computer risk analysis.**

This feels like the final piece our team has been waiting for. Now we're ready for our **first official mission.**

NOW THE SUPER SIDEKICKS ARE READY TO **SAVE THE –**

Does this thing have TV?

Ah, here we go.

I'm here at Sydney Tower for the 18th annual **Very Important Summit . . .**

Bah, these summits are a waste of time!

I used to work as security at these things with Captain Perfect and **nothing ever got solved.** The leaders just spent the whole time arguing about who had the **best golf swing.**

That's odd, I don't see Captain Perfect there.

Also missing are all the other superheroes who act as their leader's bodyguards. Strange. **Very strange indeed.**

SUPER-DUPER ALERT! SUPER-DUPER ALERT!

The computer – it's found something!

41

44

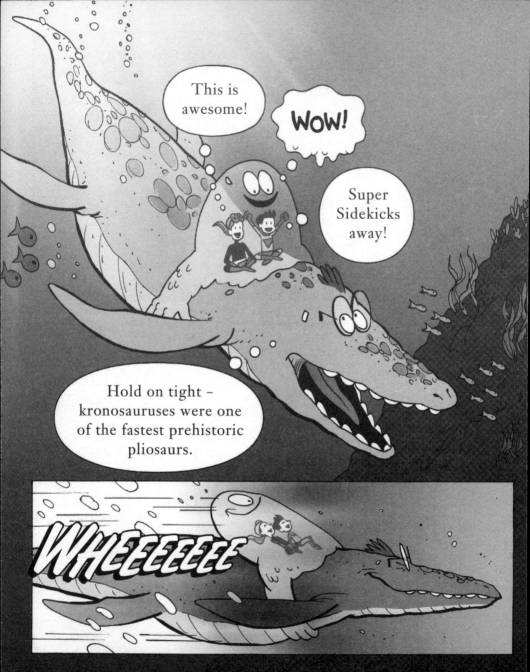

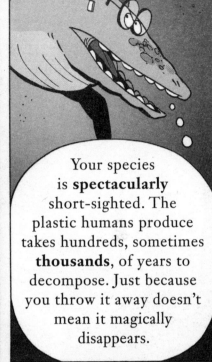

53

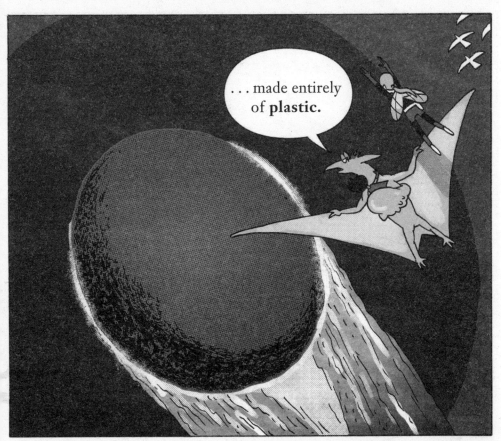

59

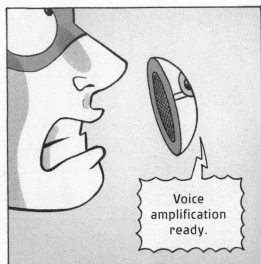

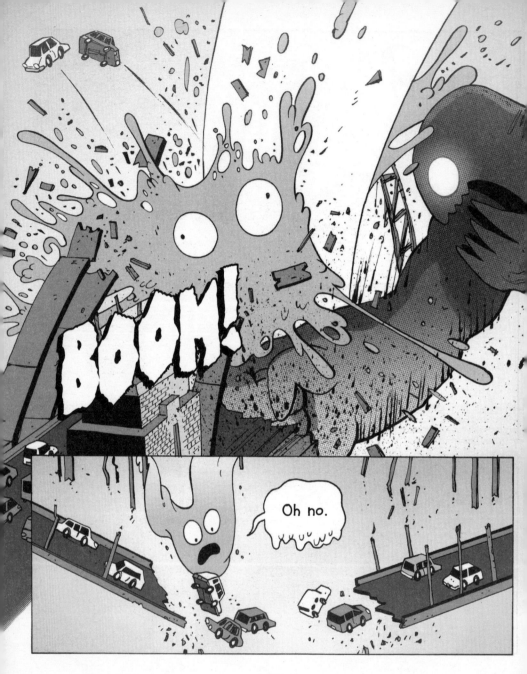

BOOM!

Oh no.

71

Chapter

One perfect,
pristine ecosystem.

And then you humans appear and think you own the entire planet.

Suddenly my home is the **dumping ground** for all of your trash.

Radioactive waste, poisonous chemicals, disgusting oil and, above all, our dreaded enemy that never dies . . .

The one you call 'PLASTIC'.

I was patient.

I gave you time to see the error of your ways. After all, I am a loving mother of **ALL** life, and you are a young civilization.

I thought no species would be careless enough to **destroy their own home.** Cutting down forests, wiping out animals and burning the ancient fossils in the ground, which suffocates the planet!

Surely no species could be so reckless. **Surely** their leaders would do something about it. **Surely** they would work together to fix it. But year after year, **you did nothing.**

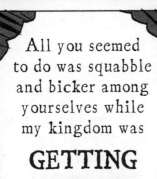

All you seemed to do was squabble and bicker among yourselves while my kingdom was

GETTING RUINED!

So do you know what happened next?

I ran out of patience. Instead, I started plotting **revenge.**

That's when I had a delightful idea: if humans want to destroy my home, then fine. I'll destroy their home too.

Humans want to fill my oceans with their plastic?

Fine — I'll use that plastic against humans. That's why I created the **Trash Titan.** Your own filth will ultimately **destroy you.**

How poetic.

HEE HEE HEE HEE HEE HEE HEE HEE

Sydney is just the first of many cities to fall. My Titan was created with only the plastic in the **PACIFIC** Ocean.

There are millions more tonnes of your junk in my other oceans that can be turned into Titans.

More Titans to destroy all of your hideous cities.

Ah, revenge is so much more satisfying than being patient!

You . . . you can't do this.

Tell me something, Mrs Prime Minister . . .

. . . who's going to stop me?

Um . . . Goo have idea.

Heh.

Spit it out, mate.

Goo **friend** with plastic thing. Goo tell friend to **stop**.

It did seem to hesitate when you spoke to it.

But plastic friend distracted. Goo need try again. **Get closer.**

You do both share similarities. Dr Enok created you in a lab, and this creature seems to be some kind of artificial being . . .

It could be serving a master like you once did, Goo. Perhaps there is a **strange connection** between you.

98

What about Ada's **mental link thingy?** Would that help?

Good idea! Ada, can it be done?

In theory, yes. I can translate any language in the universe.

Though I would have to be placed in an **optimal position**, between the creature's eyes, for any chance of success.

We have to try!

It would be an exciting experiment in linguistics.

But how are we going to get Goo close enough?

101

108

No . . . don't see you in here.

H.E.R.O. GUIDE BOOK

You probably missed the registration date.

No, I paid the fee and everything.

JUNIOR JUSTICE!

Thank goodness, our sidekicks are here. They'll handle this!

You let your sidekicks form their own team? **You can't be serious.**

They don't stand a chance!

JJ, you're hit!

I'm not that stressed, Flygirl.

See, I don't have any powers for this thing to feed on.

You're just . . . a **civilian?**

A civilian who's dedicated his life to mastering the martial arts . . .

POP!

TICKLE TICKLE

. . . including **Mongolian tickle fighting!**

STOP! STOP!

You should probably turn around now.

FHOOF!

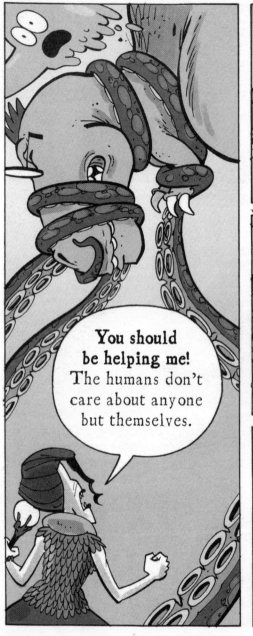

You should be helping me! The humans don't care about anyone but themselves.

SCHLONK!

FHOOF!

OW!

Can't transform! Blast this infernal *Asteroidea**.

* That's the scientific term for 'starfish'.

LAUNCH!

99.9% probability of sceptre's position acquired. Throw your staff at my target with maximum strength . . .

. . . in 4, 3, 2, 1.

127

You have **one year.** Or the Trash Titans will return.

Understood.

And I have one more condition. These world leaders must help with the cleaning themselves. **One hundred tonnes of plastic each.**

What?!

She's mad!

Can't my vice-president do it?

DEAL!

Chapter 6

143

147

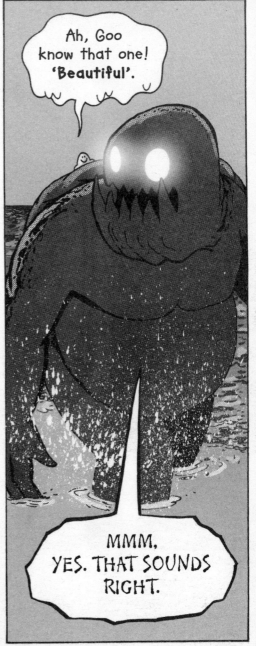

151

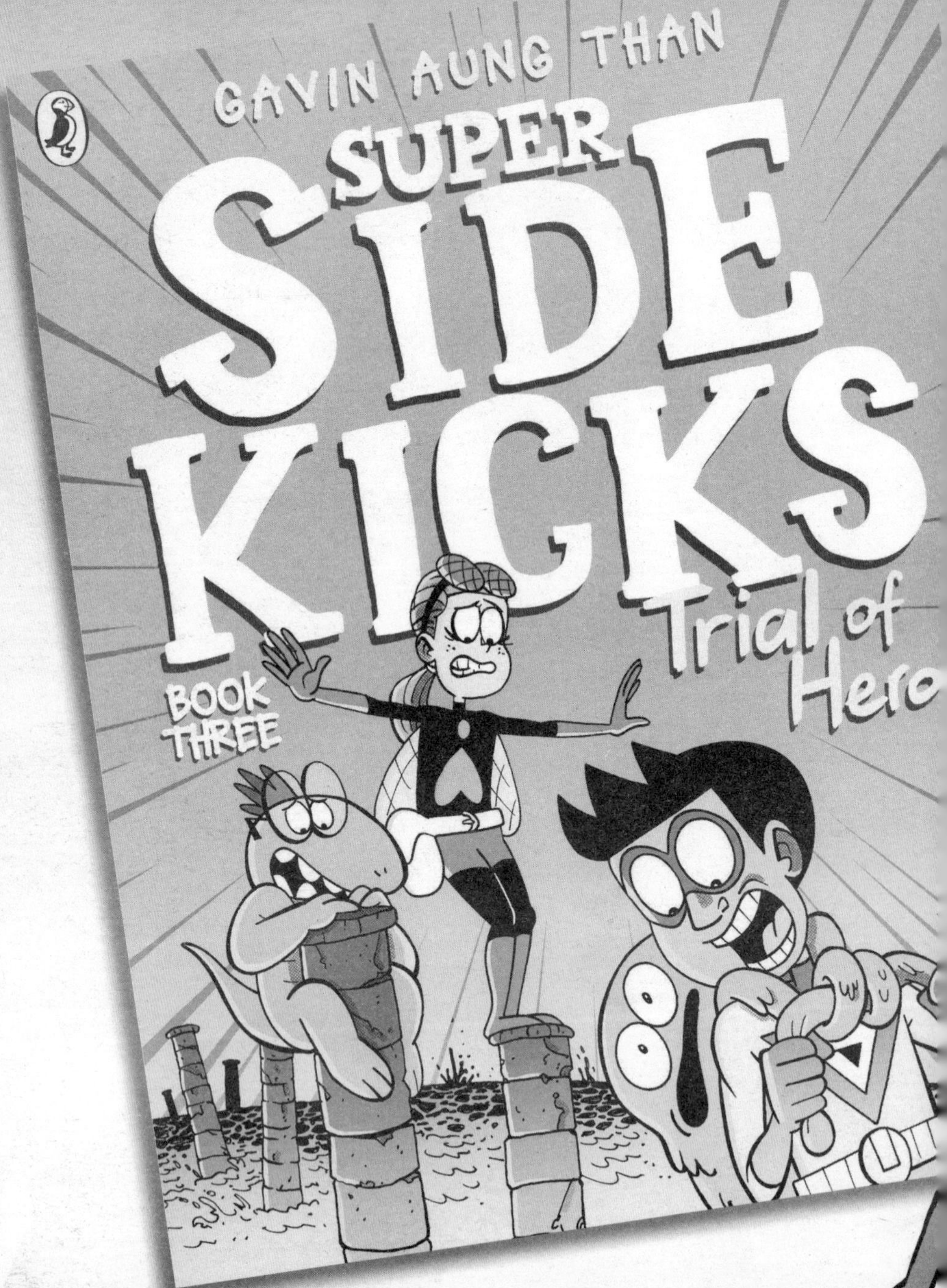
GAVIN AUNG THAN
SUPER SIDEKICKS
BOOK THREE
Trial of Hero

Don't worry,
the Super Sidekicks will be back!

The Super Sidekicks just saved the world and now they've been invited to join H.E.R.O. – the Heroic Earth Righteousness Organization – an exclusive club for the planet's most famous superheroes. But before they can become members, the team must first pass the hardest challenge in the universe, a test so scary and difficult only the truly heroic can survive.

COMING SOON – SUPER SIDEKICKS 3:

Trial of Heroes

Sounds like a must-read, chums!

HOW TO DRAW THE
SUPER SIDEKICKS

Gav's tips:

- **START WITH SIMPLE SHAPES FIRST.** For instance, JJ is just made of circles and rectangles.

- **DON'T DRAW TOO DARK.** Sketch lightly first until you get the basic structure right.

- **ONE STEP AT A TIME.** Once you have the structure done, then it's time to draw all the cool details.

- **JUST HAVE FUN.** Don't worry if you think you're not getting it right. Keep practising – it takes time to get good!

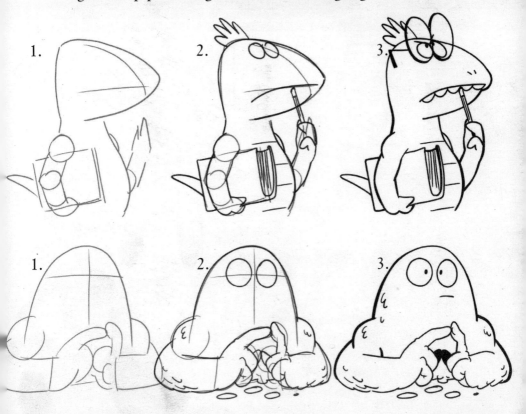

GAVIN AUNG THAN is a *New York Times* bestselling cartoonist and the creator of the Super Sidekicks. Gavin grew up loving to draw superheroes and now, as an adult, gets to draw superheroes for a job. He's sure it's some kind of mistake.

• Visit Gav's website at *AUNGTHAN.COM*
• Follow *@SUPERSIDEKICKS.OFFICIAL* on Facebook or Instagram for behind-the-scenes content and the latest Super Sidekicks news.